Camping Out

Heather Amery

Illustrated by Stephen Cartwright

Language consultant: Betty Root
Series editor: Jenny Tyler

There is a little yellow duck to find on every page.

This is Apple Tree Farm.

This is Mrs. Boot, the farmer. She has two children, called Poppy and Sam, and a dog called Rusty.

A car stops at the gate.

A man, a woman and a boy get out.
"Hello," says the man. "May we camp on your farm?"

"Yes, you can camp over there."

"We'll show you the way," says Mr. Boot.
The campers follow in the car.

The campers put up their tent.

Poppy and Sam help them. They take chairs,
a table, a cooking stove and food out of the car.

Then they all go to the farmhouse.

Mrs. Boot gives the campers a bucket of water
and some milk. Poppy and Sam bring some eggs.

"Can we go camping?"

"Please Dad, can we put up our tent too?"
says Poppy. "Oh yes, please Dad," says Sam.

Mr. Boot gets out the tent.

Poppy and Sam try to put up the little blue tent
but it keeps falling down. At last it is ready.

"Come and have supper."

"Then you can go to the tent," says Mrs. Boot.
"But you must wash and brush your teeth first."

Poppy and Sam go to the tent.

"It's not dark yet," says Sam. "Come on, Rusty.
You can come camping with us," says Poppy.

Poppy and Sam go to bed.

They crawl into the tent and tie up the door.
Then they wriggle into their sleeping bags.

"What's that noise?"

Sam sits up. "There's something walking around outside the tent," says Sam. "What is it?"

Poppy looks out of the tent.

"It's only Daisy, the cow," she says. "She must have strayed into this field. She's so nosy."

Daisy looks into the tent.

Rusty barks at her. Daisy is scared. She tries to
back away but the tent catches on her head.

Daisy pulls at the tent.

She pulls it down and runs off with it. Rusty chases
her. Poppy and Sam run back to the house.

Mr. Boot opens the door.

"Hello, Dad," says Sam. "Daisy's got our tent."
"I think camping is fun," says Poppy.

Cover design by Hannah Ahmed   Digital manipulation by Nelupa Hussain
This edition first published in 2004 by Usborne Publishing Ltd, 83-85 Saffron Hill, London EC1N 8RT, England. www.usborne.com